I Want a Pet

Lauren Child

TRICYCLE PRESS

Berkeley, California • Toronto

I *really* want a pet.

"Please Mom, can I have a pet?"
Mom says, "Well, perhaps something
with not too much fur."
Dad says, "Maybe something that lives outside."
Granny says, "Nothing with a buzz." It interferes
with her hearing aid.
Grandad says, "Stuffed pets are very reliable."

The pet shop lady says, "Goldfish can be fun."

I say, "How?"

Mom asks, "What sort of pet would you like?"
I say, "How about an African lion? I'd train him and we could do a show. We'd be a roaring success."

Granny says, "Lions have a habit of snacking between meals."

I think, uh-oh...

"A sheep would be nice, and they're vegetarian.
We could knit sweaters together."

Grandad says, "Sheep are forever following you around. They don't have minds of their own."

I hate copycats.

"How about a wolf? I bet they have lots of good ideas.
And wolves are good sniffers, so we'd never get lost."

Dad says, "Wolves are also good at howling.
Howling gives me a headache."

Dad isn't much fun when he's got a headache.

"Maybe an octopus is the answer. They're quiet, and we could go diving in the tub."

Mom says, "Do you have any idea how many footprints an octopus would make?"
I say, "Eight."

Mom says, "Exactly."

"A boa constrictor would be perfect. They don't have legs, and they hardly make a sound."

Dad says, "Boa constrictors have a habit of wrapping themselves around you and squeezing too tightly."

Maybe I want a pet that's a bit less friendly.

"How about a bat? At night we could flap around, and during the day we'd dangle upside down in the closet."

Mom says, "If anyone mentions bats in the closet, there'll be no chocolate éclairs!"

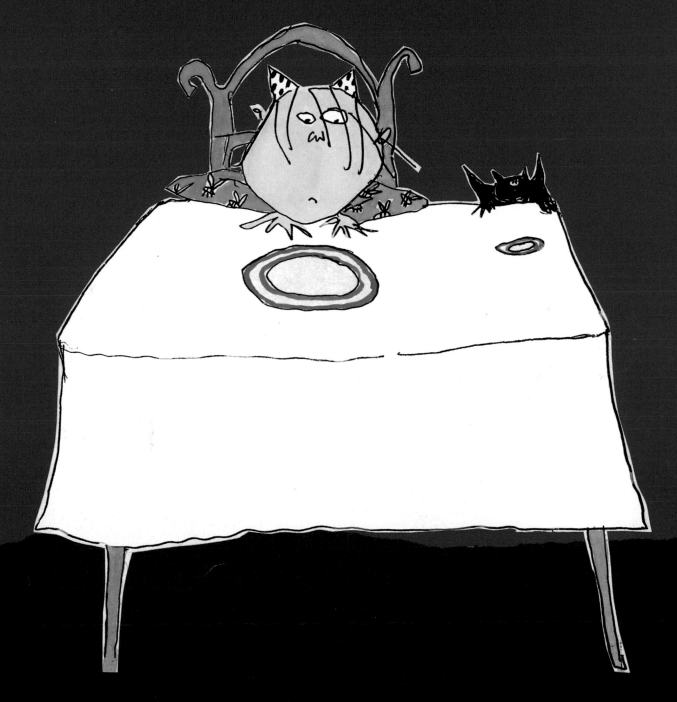

Chocolate éclairs are my favorite.

So I must try and find a pet that
won't eat me,
won't copy my ideas,
won't make too much noise,

won't leave dirty footprints around the house,
won't squeeze me too hard,
and won't make my mom so mad, she cancels
chocolate éclairs.

The pet shop lady says she can think of one thing that doesn't leave footprints, doesn't eat, doesn't move and doesn't make a peep.

No one's exactly sure what it is, because it's not quite a pet yet...

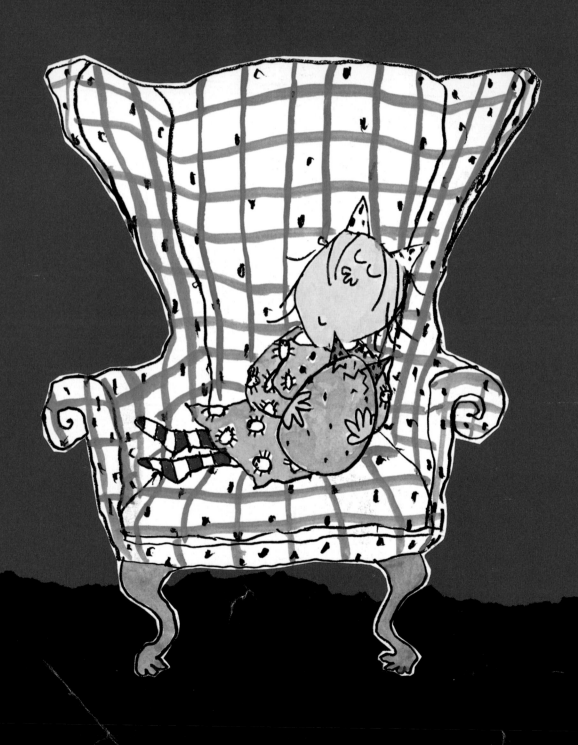

but it will be soon.